In My Anaana's Amautik

To my children, Kian and Ria. Without you, I would not be me: a mother, yours and foremost. Kian, I thank you for sharing with me your ideas and your memories of what it's like to be in "Anaana's amautik." Ria, you bring so much joy and love to our lives. To all mothers and guardians: I dedicate this to you. Without you, a child could not experience the feelings that come with being in Anaana's amautik.

Published by Inhabit Media Inc.
www.inhabitmedia.com

Inhabit Media Inc. (Iqaluit) P.O. Box 11125, Iqaluit, Nunavut, X0A 1H0
(Toronto) 191 Eglinton Avenue East, Suite 310, Toronto, Ontario, M4P 1K1

Editors: Neil Christopher and Grace Shaw
Art director: Danny Christopher

This project was made possible in part by the Government of Canada.

We acknowledge the support of the Canada Council for the Arts for our publishing program.

Printed in Canada

Library and Archives Canada Cataloguing in Publication

Title: In my anaana's amautik / by Nadia Sammurtok ; illustrated by Lenny Lishchenko.
Names: Sammurtok, Nadia, author. | Lishchenko, Lenny, illustrator.
Identifiers: Canadiana 20190137096 | ISBN 9781772272529 (hardcover)
Classification: LCC PS8637.A5384 I5 2019 | DDC jC813/.6-dc23

In My Anaana's Amautik

by Nadia Sammurtok

illustrated by
Lenny Lishchenko

In my *anaana's amautik*, I feel warm. The warmth of her skin feels like sunshine, keeping me safe from the cold. I love being in my anaana's amautik.

In my anaana's amautik, it feels cozy. The way the material swaddles me feels like being wrapped up in soft clouds. I love snuggling up inside my anaana's amautik.

In my anaana's amautik, I feel calm. Her scent reminds me of flowers in the summertime. I love breathing in the smell of my anaana's amautik.

In my anaana's amautik, it feels soft. The fabric inside it feels like a bed of cottongrass. I love curling up inside my anaana's amautik.

In my anaana's amautik, I feel safe. The protection of the hood around me is like my own tiny *iglu*. I love peeking out from inside my anaana's amautik.

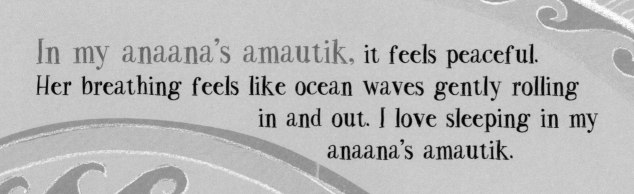

In my anaana's amautik, it feels peaceful.
Her breathing feels like ocean waves gently rolling
in and out. I love sleeping in my
anaana's amautik.

In my anaana's amautik, I feel happy. The sound of her laughter is like a glistening stream trickling by. I love playing in my anaana's amautik.

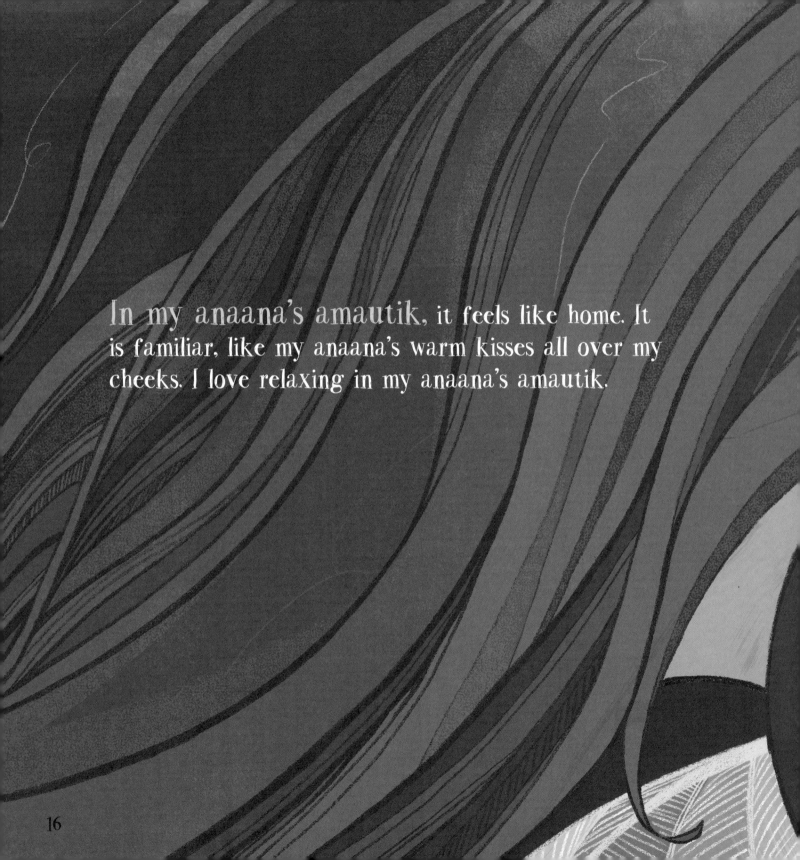

In my anaana's amautik, it feels like home. It is familiar, like my anaana's warm kisses all over my cheeks. I love relaxing in my anaana's amautik.

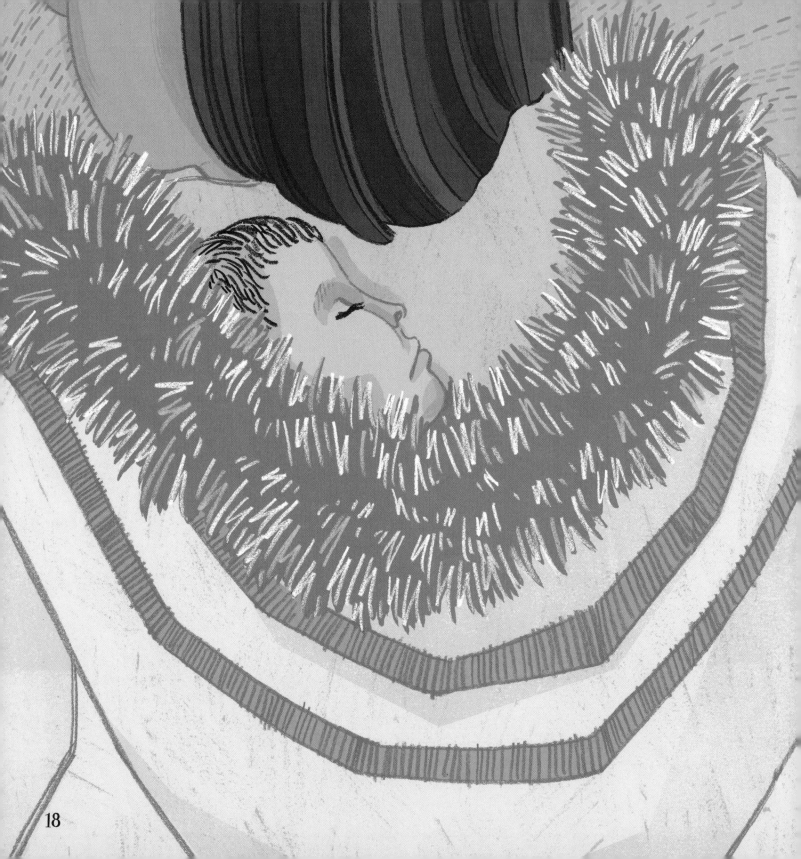

In my anaana's amautik, I feel loved. The gentleness of her movements reminds me of her hugs and her love for me. I love my anaana's amautik.

Glossary

For more Inuktitut pronunciation resources, including audio recordings of these terms, please visit inhabitmedia.com/inuitnipingit

anaana (a-NAA-na): mother

amautik (a-MOW-tick): the pouch in the back of a woman's parka where a baby can be carried

iglu (IG-loo): snow house

Nadia Sammurtok is an Inuit writer and educator originally from Rankin Inlet, Nunavut. Nadia is passionate about preserving the traditional Inuit lifestyle and Inuktitut language so that they may be enjoyed by future generations. Nadia currently lives in Iqaluit, Nunavut, with her family.

Lenny Lishchenko is not a boy. She is an illustrator, graphic designer, and comics maker who will never give up the chance to draw a good birch tree. Ukrainian-born and Canadian-raised, she's interested in telling stories that people remember years later, in the early mornings, when everything is quiet and still. She is based out of Toronto, Ontario.

Inhabit Media Inc.

Iqaluit · Toronto